The Night Before Christmas

Clement C. Moore

Illustrated by Bill Bell

Derrydale
New York

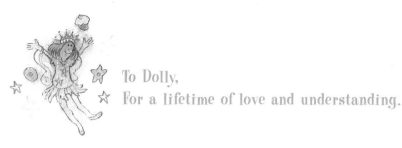

To Dolly,
For a lifetime of love and understanding.

The Night Before Christmas

This 2004 edition is published by Derrydale Books, an imprint of Random House Value Publishing,
a division of Random House, Inc., New York, by arrangement with Lionheart Books, Ltd.

Derrydale Books is a registered trademark and the colophon is a trademark of Random House, Inc.

Design: Carley Wilson Brown
Project Manager: Deb Murphy

Random House
New York · Toronto · London · Sydney · Auckland
www.randomhouse.com

Printed and bound in China

A catalog record for this title is available from the Library of Congress.

ISBN 0-517-22339-2

10 9 8 7 6 5 4 3 2 1

'Twas the night before Christmas,

When all through the house, not a creature was stirring,

Not
even
a mouse.

The stockings were hung by the chimney with care, in hopes that St. Nicholas soon would be there.

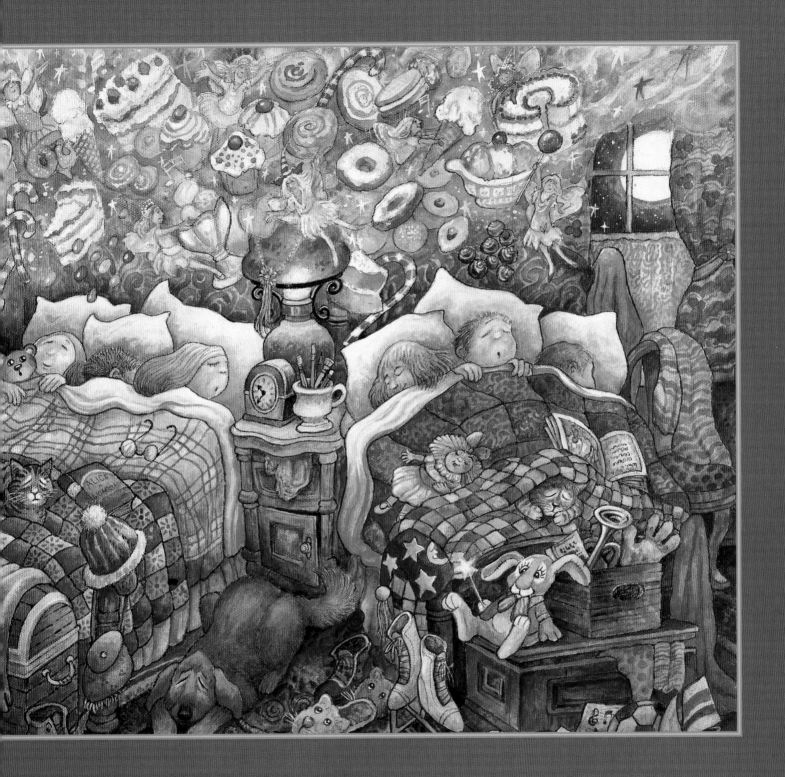

The children were nestled all snug in their beds,
While visions of sugarplums danced in their heads;

And mamma
in her kerchief,
and I in my cap,
had just settled down
for a long winter's nap,

When out on the lawn there arose such a clatter, I sprang from my bed to see what was the matter. Away to the window I flew like a flash, tore open the shutters and threw up the sash.

The moon on the breast
of the new-fallen snow
gave the luster of midday
to objects below,

When what to my wondering eyes should appear, but a miniature sleigh, and eight tiny reindeer, with a little old driver, so lively and quick, I knew in a moment it must be St. Nick!

More rapid than eagles

his coursers they came,

and he whistled,

and shouted, and

called them by name:

"Now, Dasher! Now, Dancer!

Now, Prancer and Vixen!

On, Comet! On, Cupid!

On Donner and Blitzen!

To the top of the porch!

To the top of the wall!

Now dash away!

Dash away!

Dash away,

all!"

As dry leaves

that before the wild

hurricane fly,

when they meet with

an obstacle,

mount to the sky,

so up to the housetop

the coursers they flew,

with the sleigh full

of toys, and

St. Nicholas, too.

And then, in a twinkling, I heard on the roof the prancing and pawing of each little hoof. As I drew in my head, and was turning around, down the chimney St. Nicholas came with a bound.

He was dressed
all in fur, from his head
to his foot, and his
clothes were all tarnished
with ashes and soot;
a bundle of toys he had
flung on his back, and
he looked like a peddler
just opening his pack.

His eyes,
how they twinkled!
His dimples, how merry!
His cheeks
were like roses,
his nose like a cherry!

His droll little mouth
was drawn up like a bow,
and the beard
on his chin was
white as the snow;

The stump of a pipe
he held tight in his teeth,
and the smoke,
it encircled his head
like a wreath.

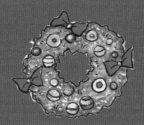

He had a broad face and
a little round belly
that shook when he laughed,
like a bowl full of jelly.

He was chubby
and plump, a right jolly
old elf, and I laughed
when I saw him,
in spite of myself.

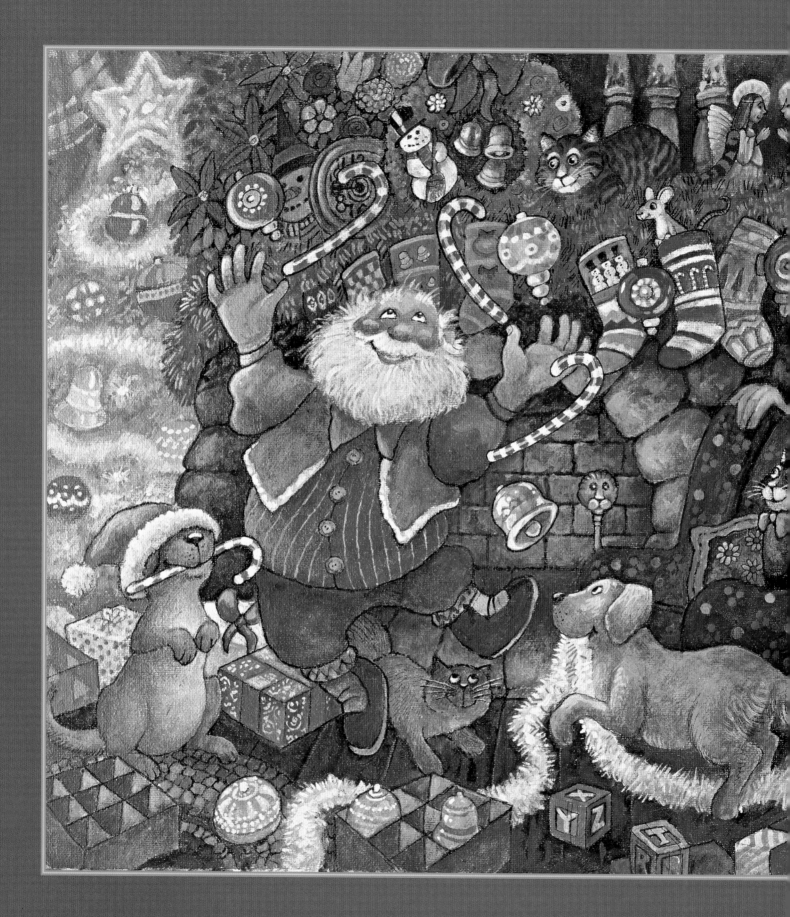

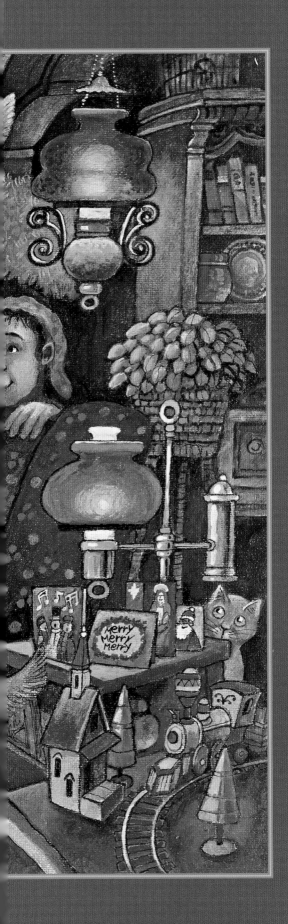

A wink of his eye
and a twist
of his head, soon gave
me to know I had
nothing to dread.

He spoke not a word,
but went straight to his work,
and filled all the stockings;
then turned with a jerk,

And laying his finger aside of his nose,
and giving a nod,

Up the chimney he rose.

He sprang
to his sleigh,
to his team
gave a whistle,

and away they all flew
like the down
of a thistle.

But I heard him exclaim,
ere he drove out of sight,
"Happy Christmas to all,
and to all a Good Night!"

The End